Tasha Tudor's

ADVENT CALENDAR

A Wreath of Days

Philomel Books
New York

*To Trudy,
Fenton, & Toby
with love, Fenwick
Dave & Alison*

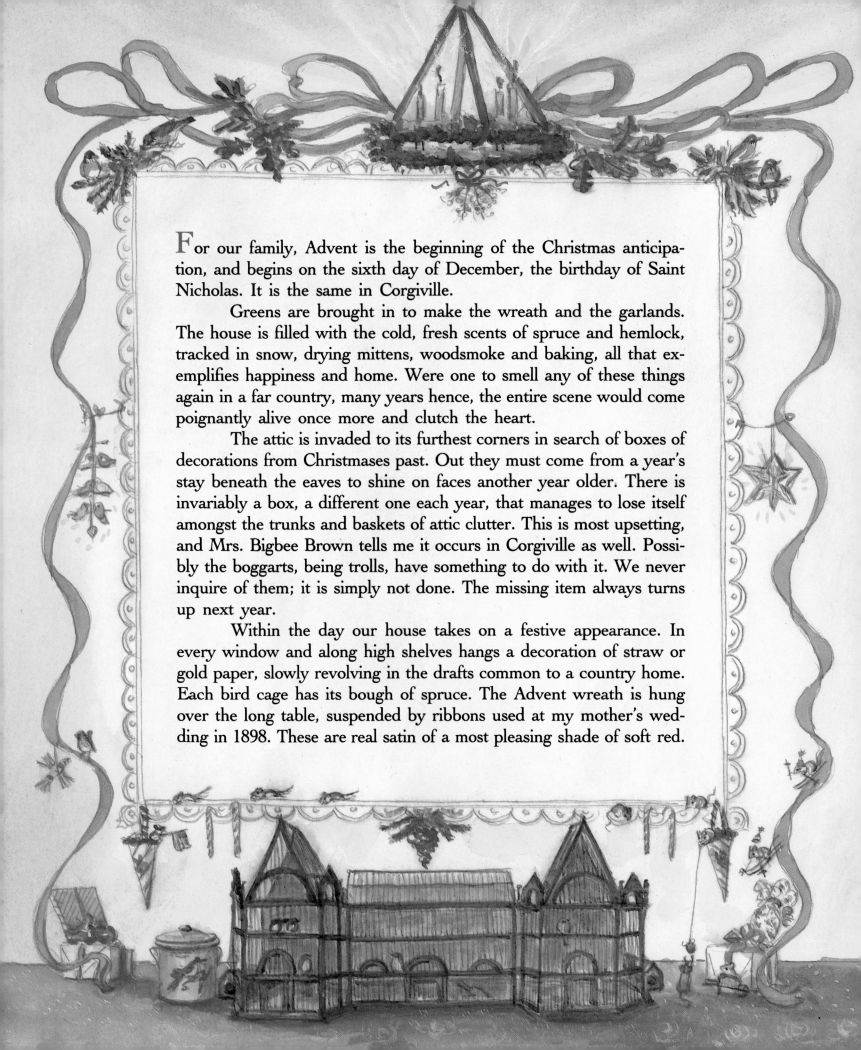

For our family, Advent is the beginning of the Christmas anticipation, and begins on the sixth day of December, the birthday of Saint Nicholas. It is the same in Corgiville.

Greens are brought in to make the wreath and the garlands. The house is filled with the cold, fresh scents of spruce and hemlock, tracked in snow, drying mittens, woodsmoke and baking, all that exemplifies happiness and home. Were one to smell any of these things again in a far country, many years hence, the entire scene would come poignantly alive once more and clutch the heart.

The attic is invaded to its furthest corners in search of boxes of decorations from Christmases past. Out they must come from a year's stay beneath the eaves to shine on faces another year older. There is invariably a box, a different one each year, that manages to lose itself amongst the trunks and baskets of attic clutter. This is most upsetting, and Mrs. Bigbee Brown tells me it occurs in Corgiville as well. Possibly the boggarts, being trolls, have something to do with it. We never inquire of them; it is simply not done. The missing item always turns up next year.

Within the day our house takes on a festive appearance. In every window and along high shelves hangs a decoration of straw or gold paper, slowly revolving in the drafts common to a country home. Each bird cage has its bough of spruce. The Advent wreath is hung over the long table, suspended by ribbons used at my mother's wedding in 1898. These are real satin of a most pleasing shade of soft red.

It is impossible to describe the beautiful effect of firelight and candlelight glinting from the decorations and casting shadows on the white-washed walls. Years of homemade Advent calendars are tacked to the length of wall behind the table awaiting the opening of the doors numbered six. The great wreath makes a shadow halo of quivering rays on the white ceiling. The smell of greens and wood-smoke is delicious. In the stillness of that first glimpse, one of the canaries will often trill into song beneath his cage cover. The birds must feel it is a hallowed time.

From the sixth until the twenty-fourth, every evening sees the lighted wreath and each day a door is opened on the many calendars. Of course, everyone gets a turn since there are so many. Invariably the boys choose the boggart calendars; these are decidedly family affairs, never published, since they are very naughty. Some doors have been known to contain small flat gifts concealed within; you never know what to expect.

Between the sixth and the twenty-fourth, Christmas presents have to be finished and wrapped, boxes of special Christmas cookies packed, treats prepared for all the animals and birds.

There never is enough time to do everything one wishes, but then this is all part of the exciting bustle of Advent. There are few events so satisfying as the pleasurable anticipation of the coming Christmas in the silence of cold and snow without, and the warmth and happiness within.

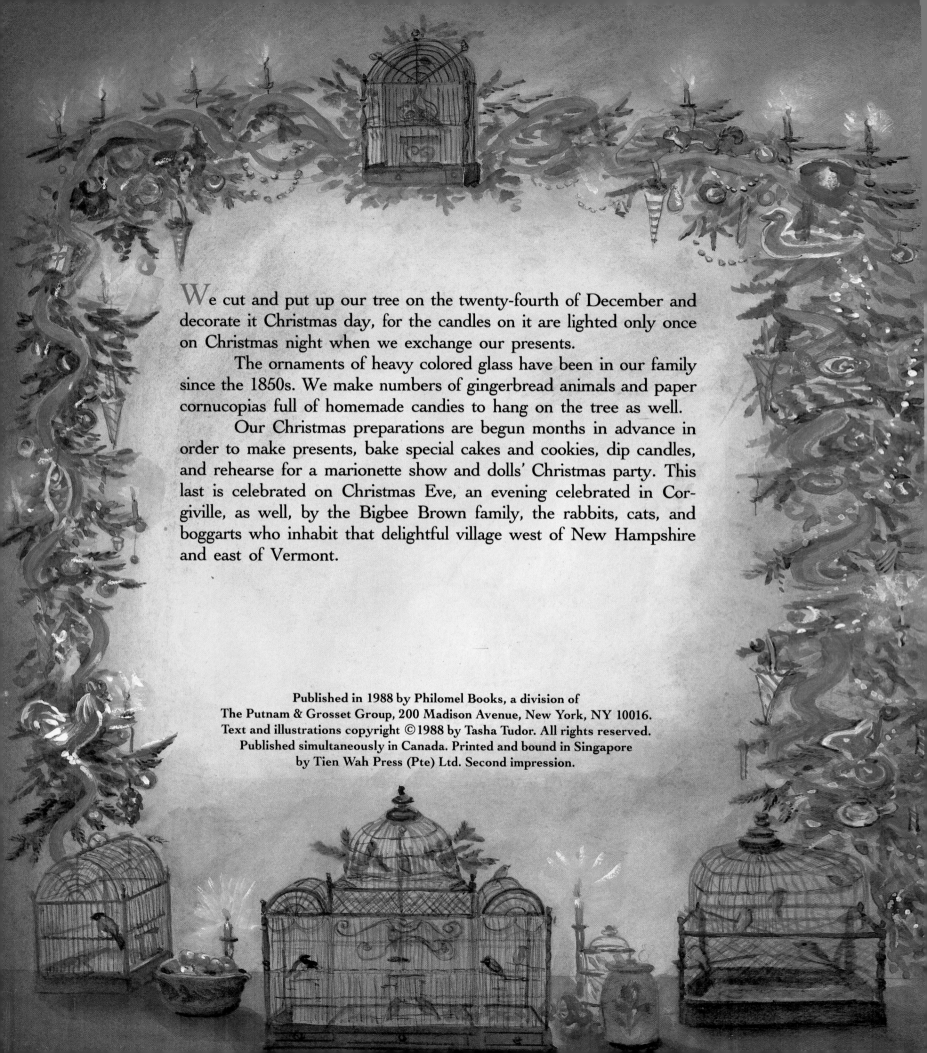

We cut and put up our tree on the twenty-fourth of December and decorate it Christmas day, for the candles on it are lighted only once on Christmas night when we exchange our presents.

The ornaments of heavy colored glass have been in our family since the 1850s. We make numbers of gingerbread animals and paper cornucopias full of homemade candies to hang on the tree as well.

Our Christmas preparations are begun months in advance in order to make presents, bake special cakes and cookies, dip candles, and rehearse for a marionette show and dolls' Christmas party. This last is celebrated on Christmas Eve, an evening celebrated in Corgiville, as well, by the Bigbee Brown family, the rabbits, cats, and boggarts who inhabit that delightful village west of New Hampshire and east of Vermont.

Published in 1988 by Philomel Books, a division of
The Putnam & Grosset Group, 200 Madison Avenue, New York, NY 10016.
Text and illustrations copyright © 1988 by Tasha Tudor. All rights reserved.
Published simultaneously in Canada. Printed and bound in Singapore
by Tien Wah Press (Pte) Ltd. Second impression.